WOMAN

WOMAN

by
Wendy Jett

Accents Publishing • Lexington, Kentucky • 2025

Accents Publishing
Editor: Katerina Stoykova-Klemer
Cover Art: Stevie Sidney

Library of Congress Control Number: 2025945932
ISBN: 978-1-961127-19-7
First Edition

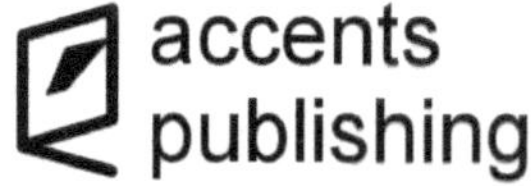

Accents Publishing is an independent press for brilliant voices. For a catalog of current and upcoming titles, please visit us on the Web at

www.accents-publishing.com

Contents

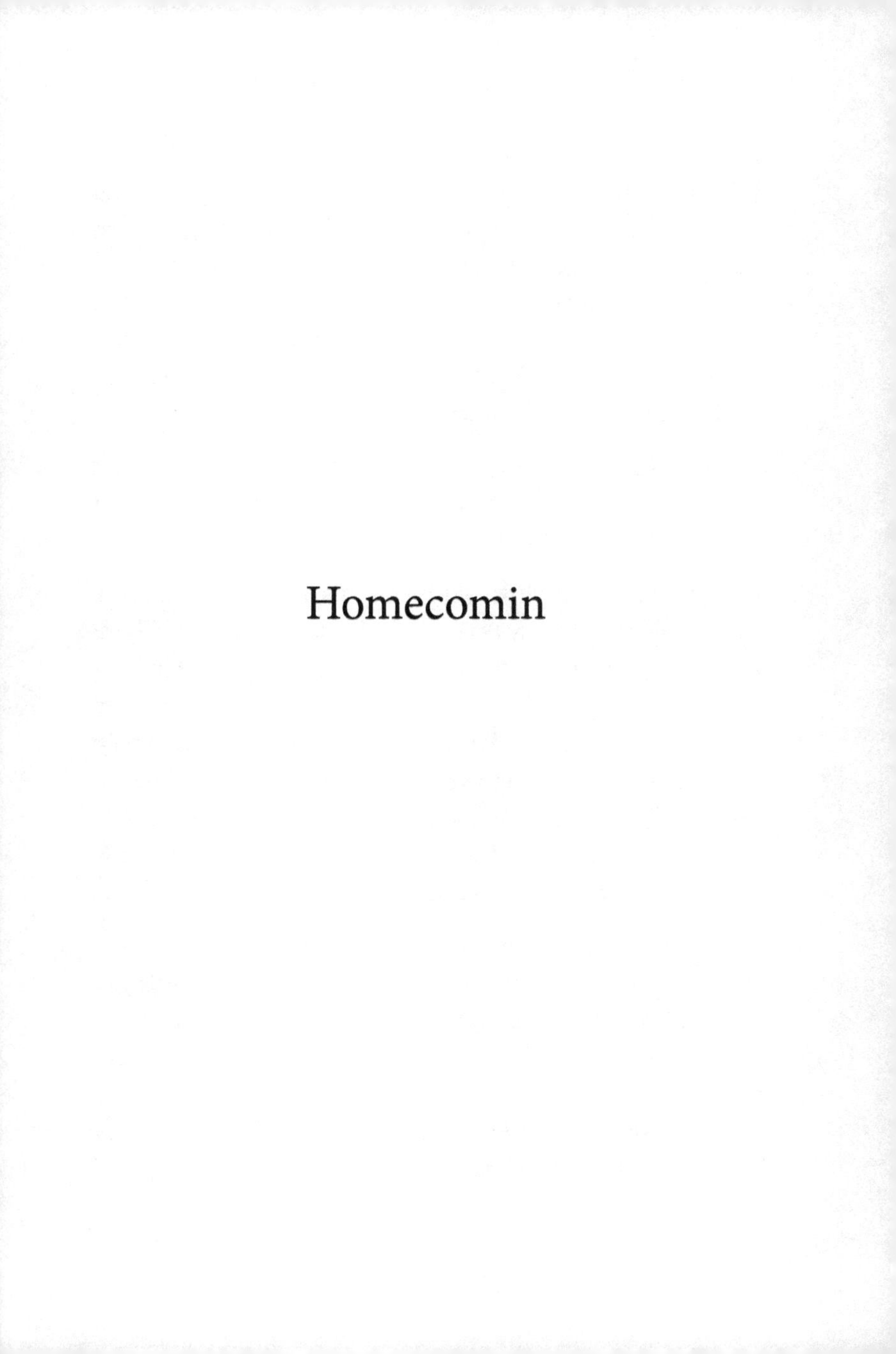

Homecomin

Lordy! I forgot how dark these roads can be. I guess I shoulda put new wipers on. They are just flappin round in the water. Can't see two feet in fronta the car. Good thing I've walked and drove these roads many a time, otherwise I woulda already been upside down in the creek! God has opened the faucet full and clean. I can't remember when it's rained this hard. Gotta turn my radio off so I can concentrate on drivin.

What's that! Oh Lord, stop stop stop! No no no! Get outta the way! Stop! Stop! Stop! Lord, please say I didn't hit it! Tell me I didn't hit it.

I throw the car in park and hit my flasher button. I think I hit it, please say it wasn't a dog. Please not a dog. There it is. Layin in the mud right in fronta the car. I think it's a possum. Maybe it's just playin possum. Hey there. Hey there. It's ok little one, don't be hissin at me. I'm gonna help ya. Well, I'll be, it's a scrawny, ugly little dog! Soaked to the bone. What do you think you're doin runnin round in this weather? Are you ok? Did I hit you little one? Now, now don't fret, I'll take care a you. Let's get ourselves in the car.

Shew! Don't be growlin at me, I'm tryin ta help ya! I don't think you're hurt. Maybe just scared to death. Let's get you and me dried off. You are an ugly little thing aren't you? I've seen many a dog in my life, but not one like you. Oh Lord what a way to start the holidays! Let's sit here a spell til the rain quiets. Just settle yourself down in my sweatshirt there in the seat.

I tell you this cold rain jumpin off the leaves and grass sure does smell like home. I bet Mama's sittin on the porch, a wrap round her shoulders listenin to the rain. Coffee still brewin. That woman can drink coffee any time of the day or night.

Can't believe it's been seven months since I seen Mama. Sometimes it feels like it was yesterday. Sometimes it feels like it's been a lifetime. She's not gonna be happy when I tell her I'm not goin back to school. I know she was countin on me bein the first one to graduate from a college, but I just miss home too much. I've tried it for goin on three years now. There's just too many people wanderin round in the city and not enough woods to get lost in. I sure hope she forgives me. That's somethin my Mama's really good at. Forgivin.

I see headlights in the mirror, sure hope they see my flashers through this rain. Now what are they doin? Slowin down and stoppin. Don't you fret, little one. I'm sure they just wanna see if they can help. People in this parta the world are good people. I roll my winda down and a man comes round the side.

"Well, well, well." He steps up to my winda. "If it ain't my Girl. What choo doin so close to home? I heard you was away at school somewhere. Whatcha got there? A possum? You always was findin the broke down things in the world."

Daddy.

"Looks like you ain't gonna make it home with them wipers. You best git in the truck and I'll take you home to your Mama." Daddy pulls on the door handle. The door opens, he starts to reach in.

"I'm not goin anywhere with you." I grab the door. "You just go on and get in your truck and be on your way. I'll be just fine til the rain stops." I try to pull the door closed but Daddy stands in the way.

"Now git yourself out here. It's gonna git cold and you can't run that engine forever. I'm gettin soaked. Git on outta that car Girl." Daddy grabs me by the arm and pulls me out. Before I know it we are standin toe to toe. Rain pourin down.

I jerk my arm away and yell, "I'm not goin anywhere with you Daddy, and don't put your hands on me! I will tell you right now, you're not gettin anywhere close to that little dog either."

"C'mon now Girl. I'm just tryin to help ya. Your Mama won't be happy with you sittin out here on a dark road. I'll give you a ride home and you can come git your car tomorra." Daddy puts his arm over my shoulder.

I push Daddy's arm off. "Don't be actin like you're doin me a favor Daddy! I don't think you've been good to me one daya my life. I'm not goin with you and stop touchin me!" I slide back into the car and slam the door.

Daddy taps on the winda. I turn and stare right at him. My breath starts to steam up the glass. I can feel Daddy's eyes burnin a hole through me but I don't say a word. I'm done talkin to that man.

Daddy puts his nose right up against the winda. "Suit yerself you stubborn, stupid Girl. I ain't beggin." Daddy walks round his truck and climbs in. I watch the blur of the tail lights fade round the corner. I'd rather freeze ta death with an ugly dog, then get in that truck with that man. It makes me even madder that I feel a hot tear slidin down my cheek.

Don't you fret little one. We will stay nice and warm til the rain stops. Let's dry you off a bit more. I'm tellin you right here and now, you stay away from that man. He already shot one dog and kicked the other one ta death. He's nobody you wanna be round. Yes, he's my daddy but he's not a good one. Let's turn the radio back on. Nothin better than some hometown music to lift your spirits. Oh no, looks like headlights comin round the bend. I hope that man isn't come back for a second go round. I've had enough. Least he could do is turn those lights off, outta my eyes.

A tap on the winda. I'm not lookin. A tap on the winda. I'm not lookin.

"Well, you best turn round here and look at me fore I hafta pull you outta a sink hole again!"

Praise be. It's BillyWade.

• *Wendy Jett*

The Night Sky

falls
into
me

settles deep for
winter's nesting

my heart swallows
black hillsides
dried knapweed

mother nature's
milk babbles
cross creek bed

floods my soul
in song

i
am
home

Notebook

Every raindrop
a teardrop
sliding
across the galaxy
of God's cheek
as he stands witness
to the day's setting sun.

Dawnin

Mama's cinnamon coffee cake swirlin round in my nose, feathers in the mattress snuggled up against my bare legs, shoulders tucked up under Granny Faye's quilts. Best way to start the day, I'd say. Been quite some time since I felt like that little girl of long ago. Life's taken a bit of a toll on my heart.

Who could Mama be atalkin to? Best not be my Daddy out there or we're gonna have ourselves a problem. Mama is so good at forgivin, but she needs to keep that man a stone's throw away.

I open the door and peep out. Mama's at the stove, cookin somethin up just talkin as fast she can, but I don't see anybody. I pull my sweatshirt over my head as I walk to the kitchen. "Good mornin Mama. Who you talkin to?"

Mama turns and I see a piece of crisp bacon ahangin outta her mouth. She tears it in half and stoops down. "Well, me and this lil possum been talkin all mornin. Ugly lil thing, but sure is sweet. She likes bacon even more than me! I don't know that I'm wanton anymore dogs round here, seein that my heart broke twice with what happened to Daisy and Huck, so if her kinfolk step up, you're gonna have ta give her back."

"I know, Mama. If she has family out there I want her to be with her kin, but til that happens we can be her family. Come here girl, com'on now. I'd say you've had enough bacon! That coffee sure smells good Mama. I think I'll have a cup. You know I think I'll just call the dog Possum. What do you think bout that Mama?"

"Sounds like a good name ta me. I don't think we'll forget it. All you gotta do is take one look at her. It's Possum. Here's ya some coffee but I didn't think you was much of a coffee drinker, Girl."

"Well, goin to college can make ya a coffee drinker real quick. All that readin and studyin. Coffee keeps ya goin in the middle of the night. But your coffee is real coffee Mama. That school coffee is like muddy water. No bite to it. That coffee cake bout done? My belly is rumblin. I gotta tell you I saw Daddy last night. He stopped when I was on the side of the road waitin for the rain to slow. He wanted to bring me home, but I didn't wanna get in that truck with him. So I didn't. Praise be that Billy Wade came along otherwise I'd be sittin there still I guess. This rain just won't stop. Cold rain too."

"Your Daddy is a stubborn man. Won't take no for an answer. Never would. I think he's bound and determined to make us a family in this house again. But I've told him we ain't doin that. You know cold winter rains bring big snows up behind em. We best make sure we got lots of wood for the fireplace in case we git ourselves snowed in here. I already asked Jack Perry ta bring me a whole load of split logs so you don't have ta worry bout doin that fore you head back ta school. He supposed to bring it by sometime today, but don't know if he'll bring it in this rain." Mama pulls the coffee cake outta the oven, sits it on toppa the stove. "Sure does smell like holidays, don't it?"

"Mama, I wanna talk to ya about school. I don't wanna go back. I wanna stay right here and help you with the house and get a job close by. School's not for me. I miss walkin in the woods and sittin at the creek. I just don't think I can do it anymore." Mama has that look in her eyes. The look of openin the chocolate candy box, and it's empty. The look she has when she runs across one of Petey's old drawins. Her eyes are surely connected right to her heart.

"Well, I was hopin you would be the first in our family to graduate from college. Me and Granny Faye both thought you'd be a good teacher. You love children and are so patient. I can't believe you don't wanna finish what you started." Mama starts to slice the coffee cake.

"Mama, I don't want to disappoint you. I'm sorry. I like school. I like learnin, but it is so hard to be away from home. People can be so mean about the way I talk, where I'm from and things like that. I just wanna be closer to home. Maybe I can be a teacher some other way. Please Mama, let me stay home awhile."

"Girl, I want you to be happy. You're the only one that knows what makes your heart happy. But I'd be lyin if I said I'm not disappointed. I am. I've always felt like you got bigger things to do in life than stayin round here.

I hope you'll change your mind in sumtime. Nuthin, nuthin is forever. I learned that a long time ago. When we make choices we think we're makin a choice for life, but it ain't so. Things change everyday. You know this is always your home. You will always belong here, Girl. There ain't nuthin, nuthin in the world you could do to make me stop lovin you and wantin you with me. I want you to think about it some more fore you make a final choice. Think about it over this school break. Now how bout a slice of this coffee cake?" Mama puts a big piece on a plate and leans over the table to give it to me. Possum jumps up outta my lap, grabs the whole piece and runs under the table.

"What in the world!" Mama yells and starts laughin. "I guess she likes coffee cake more than bacon! Ain't no use in chasin her, it's bout gone already!" Mama cuts another piece for me.

There's a knock on the door. Mama walks over and opens it. "Well, git in here! You look like a drowned well rat! C'mon in Jack. Girl, it's Jack Perry bringin the wood, pour him some coffee will ya."

I turn to see a grown man standin at the doorway. Now how could that be Jack Perry? When did little Jack Perry grow into a man as tall as the door frame?

"Well, if it ain't a girl and her possum." Jack laughs and pulls off his hat. "Thought you was more of a frog girl."

Mama's Quick Coffee Cake

1 ½ C flour
½ C sugar
2 TSP bakin powder
2 pinches salt
1 egg
½ C milk
3 TB of oil or fat

Mix all the dry ingredients together
Then add the egg, milk, oil or fat
Mix it good then pour it in a buttered dish

Make the toppin and put it on top before bakin
¼ C flour
2 TSP butter (not too soft)
2 TSP cinnamon (I like a little more)
¼ C sugar
Use a fork to chop this together so it looks like crumbles

Bake for 30 minutes at 350 degrees

• *Wendy Jett*

Scar-red

There is a rust-
ed red wagon sleep-
ing behind the barn. It no long-
er carries laughter across the yard. It-
s under belly now home to hornet's nest.

Backwoods

Been a long while since I crossed the creek to McClure's farm. Sure I haven't been there since Huck passed. I think it's time I make my way in that direction. Lots of good thinkin, healin and singin up under those pines. Still pretty wet from all that winter rain so the creek'll be up. Wasn't sure I should take Possum, but she won't take no for an answer. Got a blanket in my nap sack, gettin a bit cold out here these days.

Always feel the most at home in the woods. I love my Mama and sittin with her by the fire or on the porch, but there's nothin like listenin to the wind sing between the branches, or the smell of bits of leaves tossed in the air under your feet deep in the woods. Doesn't matter what season it is, God has touched every part of these hills with his paint brush. Bright pinks, purples and even spotted orange flowers in the spring. Summer lightnin bugs flashin yellows off and on cross the trails. Fall leaves burstin into reds like the spark offa match. Blankets of white feathered snowflakes clingin to the sides of blue gray limestone along the creek bed. God sure has a way with the woods.

C'mon Possum, you gotta keep up or I'm gonna put ya in my nap sack. Maybe that's best anyways. We're gettin close to the creek. Not sure you can jump those rocks with your scrawny little legs. C'mon now. Get your feet tucked in there.

Look right there Possum. That's where me and Huck saw all those dragonflies that day. All the angels sittin on the wings just talkin. Maybe we'll see some dragonflies one day. Today's not the day. Too cold and winter's comin. Ice'll be floatin in that water soon enough.

Don't know what's wrong with me lately. Seems I don't have the strength to climb like I used to. My legs are tired and I just feel plumb wore out. Could be all those months I spent in the city goin to school. School might make ya smart but it can also make a body lazy. Good thing I had a job in the bookstore. Kept me busy and I met a couple good friends I won't be forgettin. I'd say Hattie Maye and me will be friends forever. She grew up not too far from here, other side of Green River. She's stayin at school. Says she wants to be the first woman doctor in Green River Valley. If anybody can do that, it's her. Jessie Payne is another I won't soon forget. All those red curls huggin his head. Green eyes peepin out from under his thick brows. Smile as bright as the mornin sun. He can play anything that's got a string but that guitar, boy oh boy he can play that guitar. Got a voice like wind floatin through a cave. Takes your breath away. Said he's in school because his daddy said he had to. He's goin out west as soon as he can to make his life playin music. Sounds like a good life to me. Making music. Jessie sure stole a piece of my heart.

Shew Possum! I sure don't remember the pine trees bein this far! But we're here! Get on down and get yourself a drink. Brought some water and cornbread, you can have some. Let's get on this blanket and take a rest. Whewee, take a big whiff of those pine needles. Christmas is comin! I feel it in the air and smell it in my nose. Snuggle on in here girl. I sure am happy you showed up. I miss havin a dog around. I'm tellin you right now, you stay away from my Daddy. If he shows up you just go the other way. Takes a certain kinda meanness to mistreat a dog, and I'm tellin you, my Daddy's got that meanness down in his bones. Let's try to take a quick little nap and not think about Daddy at all.

Praise be! It's gonna be gettin dark soon, we slept too long Possum! Get up! We gotta head home! Possum. Possum. Where are ya girl? C'mon now! It's no time to be playin games! Get back here! Possum!

Possum! Where are ya? Possum!

Possum! Here girl!

Possum honey! Where are ya! Possum! Oh Lord, I can't take losin another dog.

Possum! C'mon girl! Come to me!

Where are ya? Possum!

Possum!

Possum! Possum! Please!

Praise be, there she is. Possum, what you got? Show it to me.

Possum. Give it to me. Oh Lord, you ate all the cornbread! You little sneak.

I'd say you're gonna fit in just fine around here.

• *Wendy Jett*

Mama's Cornbread

½ C bacon grease
2 eggs
1 C milk
1 C cornmeal
1 C flour
1 TB baking powder
2 pinches salt
2 TB sugar

Put the bacon grease in a cast iron skillet
Put the skillet in the oven and preheat to 400 degrees

While the oven is heating
Mix the eggs and milk together in a bowl
Then in another bowl sift the corn meal, flour, salt,
sugar and baking powder together

Mix the 2 bowls together then take the skillet out
of the oven and pour the melted bacon grease into the
cornbread mixture and stir it real good

Make sure you leave some bacon grease all round the
skillet
Then pour the cornbread mixture back into the skillet

Bake at 400 degrees for about 20 minutes
Might wanna test it with a fork or toothpick
Should come out clean

If you want to make some dessert cornbread then
you mix in some brown sugar and peeled apple bites
before baking

If you want to make some breakfast cornbread then
you mix in some crumbled cooked sausage or bacon
before baking

• *Wendy Jett*

Trauma

I have realized
there are places

so deep
inside me

even I cannot
travel there

Hitched

BillyWade is a daddy. He sure is! Ash and BillyWade got married the day we all graduated from highschool. Got married, Ash moved in with BillyWade and Ms. Verna and they've been livin together since then. It's been about three years now. Trigg Hawkins McKee was born eight months ago.

Baby Trigg looks like his mama and his daddy all at the same time. Head fulla hair as dark as midnight like his mama, but grey eyes with flecks of gold like his daddy. That boy sure is plump. Rolls of soft baby fat on his legs and arms. He looks like a loaf of bread sittin on the counter risin and fillin out.

BillyWade and Ms. Verna have been livin at Granny Faye's since Grandpap passed. They've been takin good care of the place. BillyWade's still been workin corn and soybeans in the fields. Since Ash moved in they have a garden even bigger than when Granny was there. They even have goats and chickens. They've been makin goat cheese and sellin it at Johnson's store.

BillyWade can't work on a tractor, but Ash can sure put anything back together that you put in fronta her. They are a perfect pair. Like peanut butter and honey. Ash can figure out how to make money outta most anything. She found a store up in Green River that's been sellin BillyWade's pictures he paints. She says an old couple from New York City opened a store there called The Fox's Den. They sell all kinds of things folks around here make to the people that stop from the interstate. Ash says they think BillyWade's paintins are 'quaint'. BillyWade says he doesn't care what they call them because they've been payin him good money for his paintins. I'd say they've been workin hard at makin a good life for themselves, baby Trigg and Ms. Verna.

Granny Faye would love knowin there's a baby growin up on the farm again. And a boy baby at that! Baby Trigg is sure gonna have some fun times around there. Drinkin water outta the well. Jumpin from the loft in the barn. Skippin rocks down at the creek. I sure hope he finds a best friend to share all that with. There's nothin better than a life long friend that loves you enough to pull you out of a sink hole. I know for a fact, those kind of friends are special and hard to come by.

I think if BillyWade's daddy saw him, he'd be so proud of the man he has grown into. Life hasn't been easy for him, but he sure has pulled himself up and built himself a real good life.

Love Spoon

Knife in hand, he carries himself deep into the sanctuary of the wood. Moving in the direction of the water, as Basswood is drawn to water. It does not take him long to spy the perfect specimen. He sees this as a sign. A sign that his beloved will agree to his proposal. Creating a small v-cut his decision is confirmed. Perfect. Knife in pocket, Basswood in hand he turns in the direction of the barn. He sits in the haystack as this is the holy place of first kiss. Begins to whittle. Two hours. Pull stroke. Sharpening. Three hours. Push stroke. Shavings. Four hours. Stop cut. Straight away cutting. Five hours. Details are breathtaking. Horseshoes. (Luck) Knots. (Security) A single cross. (Faith) Bells. (Marriage) Hearts. (Love) This spoon now boasts the skill of a master wood worker. A man in love. A man capable of providing for his family. Tonight he will gift this to his cherished one and her father. Most certainly to be his future wife and father in law.

Notebook

To remain kind and loving
in a cruel world is the most
powerful skill of all.

Foretellin

You stay here Possum. I gotta go talk to Granny Faye, she's standin out there by the big Oak. I'm sure that's her. You keep quiet. Don't wake Mama.

I can feel the frozen snow between my toes, but it doesn't feel cold for some reason. The air feels good and crisp against my face. "Granny, Granny! I'm so happy to see you! I've missed you Granny!" Granny Faye turns round and smiles. She's wearin the apron I made her. Light pink with tiny little flowers scattered around. "What are you doin out here in the middle of the night Granny?"

"Girl, you been on my mind and in my heart more than usual. I'm worried bout you Girl. I hear you done decided to stop goin to school. You was doin so good in all them hard classes. But I think that may be for the best." Granny Faye turns away and looks straight up in the sky. Moon seepin thru the gray clouds. "I need to tell you sumthin. There's sum things gonna be happenin round here soon. Things that might be hard to work through on your own. I want you to help your Mama and promise me you will take care of yourself too Girl."

Granny turns round to me and opens the pocket of her apron. "Anytime you need me you just take this here stone in your hand and hold it close. Talk to me and I'll hear you. I promise." Granny hands me a smooth, round yellow Jasper. Looks like it's been polished with a polishin cloth for months and months. "You keep this stone close by you and your Mama. You hold it tight when you say your prayers at night." Granny gives my hand a squeeze, and I can tell she's worried bout somethin.

"What's gonna happen Granny Faye?" I can hear my voice shakin. "You can tell me. What's gonna happen?" I'm startin to feel cold, and my ears are ringin.

Granny turns her back to me and looks up in the sky again. Moon's just about disappeared behind the cloud. "I want you to go see Doc Andrews soon. He can help ya. You tell your Mama that I said she has to take you. Tell her I'm gonna be watchin to make sure that gets done. Will you do that for me Girl?" Granny turns toward me. Her hands are folded up under her heart like she's prayin.

"Yes, Granny, yes, of course, I will do what you want me ta do." The ringin in my ears gets louder. I can feel my heart thumpin in my chest.

"Just do what I asked Girl. Everythins gonna be ok. You take care of yourself." Granny turns and starts to walk off. "I love you Girl. You be brave. I will come see you again soon."

I can't speak. My mouth won't work. The ringin in my ears and the thumpin in my chest is gettin louder and louder. I can't feel my feet. Or my legs. The moon's gone and so is Granny Faye. I feel myself stumble back against the tree. Then I feel the snow pushin into my ear. I can't get up. I'm sure I see a crow sittin up in the tree. I think he's singin a hymn. His mouth is movin like a man's mouth. My lips hurt, but the pain is far away.

Possum is barkin. Barkin. Barkin. I hear Mama yellin, but I can't get up.

"Girl! Girl! Oh, Lord! Girl!" Mama and Possum both come up on me. "You're gonna catch a death of cold out here! What you doin out here with no wrap and no shoes? Girl! Can you hear me? Oh, Lord!" Mama reaches up under my arms. "C'mon now, let's get you up and in the house!" Possum is barkin and lickin at my face.

"I was talkin with Granny Faye, Mama. She wants me to go see Doc Andrews." I push as hard as I can with my legs and press my back inta the tree. I can feel myself stand up. The ringin in my ears is leavin.

"What in the world you mean you was talkin to Granny Faye. This cold just has you out of your rightful mind. We best get you back in that house right now. Let's go!" Mama starts pullin me toward the house. I hear the snow crunchin under our feet, but I feel like I'm floatin. "You're all froze up Girl."

"I'm tellin you the truth Mama. I saw Granny Faye. She was wearin the apron I made her. She said she's been watchin over us. I promise I'm tellin the truth Mama. She gave me this." I open my hand. There sits the shiny, yellow Jasper stone. I feel my heart thumpin.

• *Wendy Jett*

Feral

they call her a savage
untamed barefoot witch running
through sharp thistle and thorn

tangled hair thick long wild
eyes closed chin tilted upward
mouth agape in crazed smile

they do not realize she is
made of paper and will soon
silently fold into a majestic bird

leaving them to spread tales
of the day she simply flew

away

Midnight

Canopy sway above
Makes me shudder

Footprints pressed in snow
Moon seeps tween branches

Gently I inhale myself to life
Yet I am still a bag of bones

Girl

Girl,

I'm writin you this letter so you can keep it and look at it when you are feelin like the world is too heavy for you. I want you to know that there ain't nuthin in this world that could happen that would make me stop lovin you. Nuthin. You were born of my body but live in my soul.

You have grown into such a strong, smart, determined woman. I can only hope that I helped you a bit long the way. I know your Granny Faye played a big part in you becomin such force a nature. I think your Grandpap helped you find your gentle, carin part. Your life has been filled with loss and had its share of meanness, but you always seem to find the sun and lift your face in that direction.

You are the one who brought me out the other side of my cancer, and you was just a little girl at the time. You are the one that made Petey feel special and loved every moment of his little short life. You are the one that was stubborn enuf to make me finally realize that Daddy ain't changin his ways. I shoulda left your Daddy a long time ago. I am so very sorry for puttin you and Petey in harms way. I hope that God will forgive me for such a cowardly decision.

You are everythin to me, my Girl.

The next months are gonna be hard, but they will also be the beginnin of the greatest adventure of your life.

I promise you, I will be there to help you. I know you are still in a bit a shock bout the whole thing, and I know you been worryin bout what others are gonna think of you. I'm tellin you right here and now, those who love you will always love you. Those that carry meanness and judgment in their hearts will always find sumthin to open their mouths about. Pay them no mind. God knows you are perfect as you are and so do I.

I believe all things happen cause they were supposed to happen that way. We might not understand it, but we can learn from it. You might be feelin that God has forgotten you, but I promise you that ain't happenin. Ever. He just might be sittin quiet right now, lettin you do some growin of your own, but he's always nearby. I think he's the one that sent Granny Faye to ya to make sure you went to see Doc Andrews. We are gonna be busy, busy bees the next few months gettin ready for this baby, so you get you some rest now. You are goin to be a wonderful Mama and I'm gonna be a Granny! Yes, I am! What an amazin Christmas present this was! A Granny!

I love you Girl,

Mama

Let Us Pray

Oh child of mine

Blood of my blood
Bone of my bone
Flesh of my flesh

Birthed from my earthly body

There is no greater love
Than what my heart holds for you

I pray you will always know this
Deep within the soul that is you

My beloved daughter
My Girl

• *Wendy Jett*

My Grandmother

carried me
before I was born

for the egg in my
mother's womb

which became me

was formed while my mother
slept in her mother's womb

Frettin

Are you there God? Can you hear me God? I'm here by the winda on my knees, just like I'm supposed to do. Can you hear me God? I gotta whisper so Mama doesn't hear me. I'm scared God. I'm scared I won't be the kind of mama this baby needs. I know you won't ask me to carry more than I can, but I'm feelin a bit tired these days God. Seems I don't get to rest too much before somethin else comes along. I'm worried about bein a good mama. I'm worried about Daddy stoppin by the house. I'm just plain worried. Mama says I can ask you to carry my worries for a while and you will. So I'm askin God. Can you do that for me? I hope you can hear me God. Are you there God? I gotta whisper so Mama doesn't hear me.

Are you there Granny? Can you hear me Granny Faye? I have my stone here in my hand. Just like you told me. Granny Faye, I gotta whisper so Mama doesn't hear me. Oh please be there Granny. I'm scared Granny. I need you to help me be strong. I'm scared to be someone's Mama. I'm afraid I won't be a good one. How am I supposed to know what to do? Mama told me we will help each other. That this baby is a blessin for both of us. She said I'm just surprised is all. That I will fall in love the second I see that baby's head of hair. I do love babies. Can't think of anything I loved more than baby Petey, that's for sure. But I'm scared Granny. I'm scared of Daddy bein this baby's Grandpap. I need you here with me Granny. I need you to hold my cheeks and look me in the eye and tell me I am a strong and kind girl. Oh, how I miss you Granny. Are you there Granny Faye? I gotta whisper so Mama doesn't hear me.

Are you there Petey? Can you hear me Petey? I gotta whisper so Mama doesn't hear me. I need you to take care of this baby there in heaven before it gets here to us. We just can't take losin another. Can you do that for me Petey? Take care of this baby so Mama can be a granny and I can be a mama. I'm gonna do my best to be lovin and kind. I sure do miss you. I hope you are spendin time with Granny Faye and Grandpap. Are you there Petey? I gotta whisper so Mama doesn't hear me.

Are you there Possum? Can you hear me Possum? I gotta whisper so Mama doesn't hear me. Snuggle in here girl. I need somebody ta talk to. We are gonna help this baby have a good life. Aren't we girl? Yes, we are. I know you were sent to me for a reason. It wasn't an accident that you stepped right in fronta my car. I'd say God started that rain and sent you to me. I just gotta have faith Possum. Faith that everything will work out like it's supposed to. I gotta have faith that the rainbow will always find its way outta the storm. We're gonna be ok aren't we Possum? Aren't we? Possum, are you listenin? I gotta whisper so Mama doesn't hear me.

Mama, is that you?

• *Wendy Jett*

Crow Weeps

she tucks her long feathered wings - curls tail down and under - presses her body into dried leaves - she is giving up - giving in - done giving - she will never be a beautiful bird - she realizes this now - she is the absence of color - emptiness - darkness - nothingness - this is what she shall always be - it is who she has always been - wind begins to stir - twigs rise swirling overhead - god weeps - how do you not know my crow - you are filled with color - red - blue - green - all united in deep love for one another - you are my night sky - that which boasts all colors in one moment - that which celebrates all that is holy - oh my dear crow how do you not know this is who you are

Notebook

You must turn your pockets inside out
to rid yourself of the thrown stones
you still carry.

Valentine

Every year as long as I can remember, Pastor John has had a Valentine Day party at the meetin hall by the church. Everybody brings somethin sweet to share, and we celebrate our love for one another. He says we are all each other's Valentine. That no one around here is alone. I like that. Pastor John is a good man. He does a good job at keepin everyone on the right path.

Besides all the sweets, the best thing at the party is the music. Lots of dancin and clappin lifts the heart. I'm prayin I have enough spirit in my legs to do some dancin tonight. Mama and me brought Thumbprint cookies and Granny's fudge. I'm hopin Ms. Verna's bringin her stack cake. Ash said she's makin some molasses bars. Baby Trigg's comin too. Looks like there's already a lot of people here. There's hardly any room to park the car.

Me and Mama get into the meetin hall and who's standin right inside the door? Jack Perry. Holdin a big ol plate of oatmeal cookies. "Hi Ladies. Thought I'd share some of these amazin cookies I made with everybody tonight." Jack smiles and gives us a wink. He walks to the big dessert table. Looks like Ms. Verna is organizin all the sweets. BillyWade and Ash must be here somewhere.

We walk over to the table to put down our cookies and fudge. I see two stack cakes on the table! Ms. Verna smiles when she sees me eyein them and says "Don't you worry Girl. I got you your own stack cake in the car. We gotta make sure you remember it fore you go home."

She and Mama start talkin and arrangin things. I see BillyWade so I start makin my way over to the other side of the room.

BillyWade is standin next to the wall, and Ash is sittin with baby Trigg. BillyWade motions to me to have a seat. "Pastor John asked me to paint some pictures for people tonight. He's callin it a Minute Masterpiece. He says I only got one minute to paint whatever somebody asks for. Not sure I can do that." BillyWade shakes his head.

"Oh you will do just fine BillyWade, get on over there," Ash says as she pats him on the back.

"Let me see that boy first." BillyWade grabs Trigg and gives him a toss in the air.

"Now watch out Billy. Trigg just ate. He'll be losin his supper all over you!" Ash stands and takes Trigg from BillyWade.

"Look at all the fun you're gonna have real soon Girl!" BillyWade gives my shoulder a squeeze and starts over to the picture table.

"Here, you wanna hold Trigg a bit?" Ash passes baby Trigg over to me. He's such a cute baby. Always smilin and kickin his legs. "You're gonna be such a good mama Girl. I can tell by the way you hold Trigg and you have such a tender heart. That makes for a good, carin mama." Ash starts to pull her hair back in a long ponytail. She looks so young to be married and have a baby, but we're the same age, so I guess she just looks that way. Lord knows, I already feel like an old woman most days.

I can see Jack Perry outta the corner of my eye, makin his way over to us. "Hi ladies." Jack tips his head to us. "I was hopin to maybe get a dance with a pretty girl tonight. I am hopin she also likes frogs and possums." Jack smiles. "Well, I don't mean to eat, I mean to care for." Jack starts shiftin his weight side to side. I can tell he's feelin a bit nervous.

Ash reaches for Trigg and turns to Jack. "Yes, you came to the right place. There's a girl right here that loves dancin, frogs and possums. Go on now Girl. Go have some fun, you deserve it." Ash squeezes my arm and motions for me to join Jack.

The music's a bit slower than I would like, but we start dancin. He's a good dancer. Smooth on his feet. He says that Granny Perry made him learn to dance so he could be her partner at the dances back in the day. "I was so sorry to hear about your Granny passin, Jack. I'm sorry I didn't reach out to you when that happened." I tip my head up to see him lookin down at me.

"Oh, don't fret over that. My Granny took care of me most of my life, but she was a hard, hard woman to be round. She was always so mad at the world for my mama dyin in that car crash. She never got over it. I'm glad that they are finally together now." Jack looks off over my shoulder. "Well, Girl, I think your daddy just came in."

Sure enough. There's Daddy makin his way to the dessert table and to Mama. "I gotta go over there. I'm sorry Jack." I let go of Jack's hand and make my way to Mama. I can smell that Daddy's been drinkin before I even get up to him. I can hear Mama tell him he needs to leave. I step around him and put myself right beside Mama.

I tell him, "You've been drinkin and you need to be leavin. Now." He doesn't even look at me, so I say it just a bit louder. "Daddy, you've been drinkin, and you need to leave! Now, Daddy!" He turns his face to me, and I can see that color changin.

"I ain't talkin to you Girl. I'm talkin to my wife right now and I ain't leavin." Daddy points his finger at me. I push Mama behind me and tell Daddy to put his finger down and get out. Course he doesn't like that much, so he steps toward me but stumbles.

About that time Jack Perry and BillyWade come out of nowhere and grab him up under his arms. "We're gonna help you out Mr. Baker. I will make sure you get home safe." Jack Perry starts pullin Daddy toward the door.

"I ain't goin nowhere with you Jack. Get offa me!" Daddy pulls his arm away from Jack and slips back onto BillyWade. "I sure as hell ain't goin with you either!" Daddy looks at BillyWade and pushes him.

Next thing I know the music's stopped and Pastor John is standin there next to Daddy. "C'mon Mr. Baker. You and me are gonna go outside and get some air." Pastor John puts his arm round Daddy. Daddy starts walkin with Pastor John.

"Bein you're a man of God, Pastor, who am I to argue with you." Daddy and Pastor John walk straight outta the door. The music starts back up.

I feel the baby move for the first time.

• *Wendy Jett*

Notebook

Daddy's gone swimmin again. Probably didn't even dip a toe in first. Just jumped in with both feet. Hit the water yellin at somebody I'm sure. Opened his big ol mouth wide like a catfish. Swallowed half that bottle of river in one gulp. Ain't come up for air yet. Sinkin like a rotted walnut. Slow and steady. Drownin himself with every sip.

Daddy never was a good swimmer.

Mama's Thumbprint Cookies

1 C soft butter
8 TB powdered sugar
2 C flour

Mix it all up til it's thick and smooth
Put one teaspoon of dough mix on the baking sheet
It should look like a little ball
Push your thumb down in the middle of the ball
Make a little dent

Bake 350 degrees for about 10 minutes
After they cool fill the thumbprint dent with icing
Fill it up real good

Icing

Powdered Sugar and milk
Just make it however thick you want

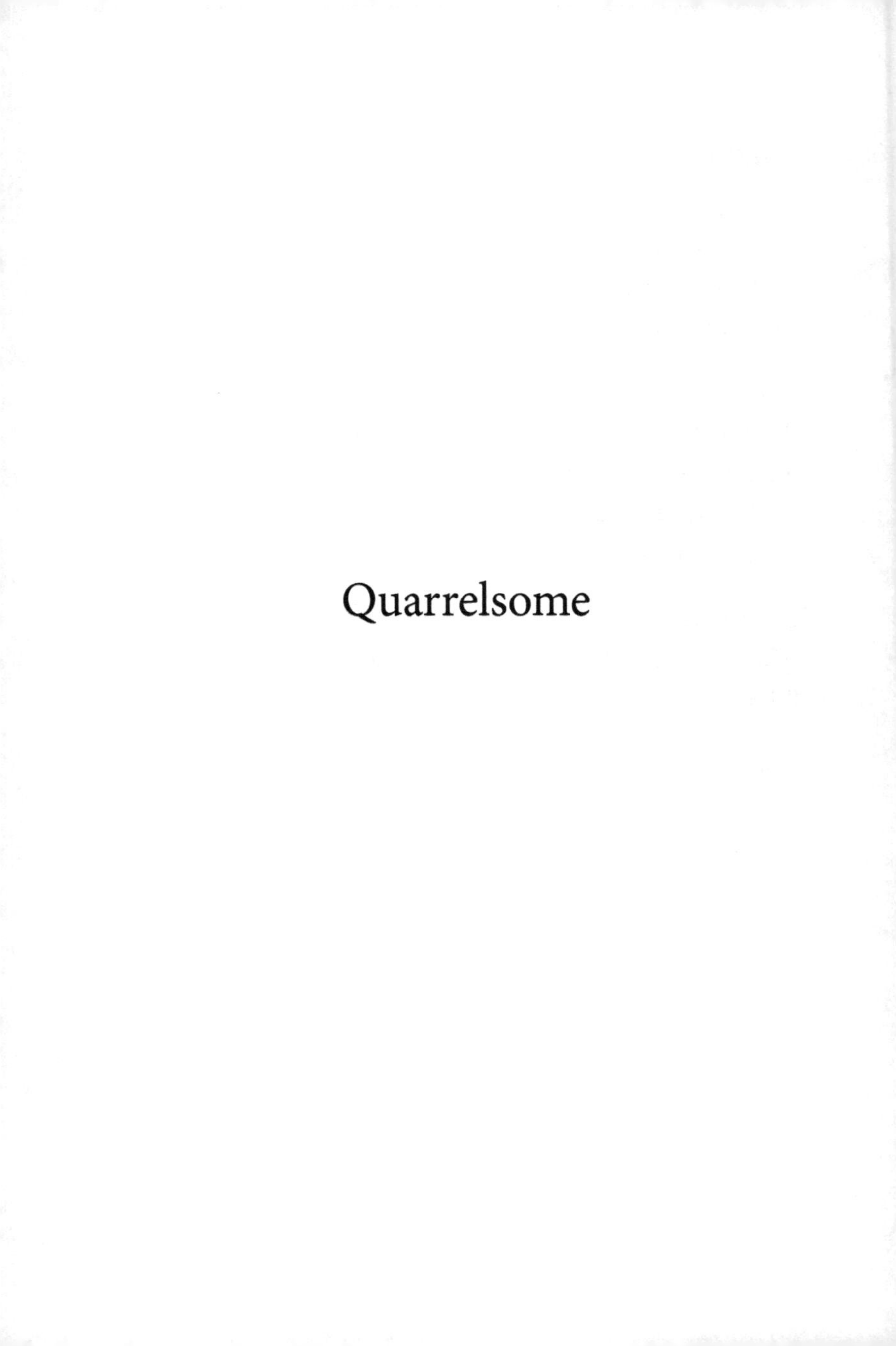

Quarrelsome

I'm not doin it Mama. I'm not. I'm not doin it. I am not gonna tell this baby's daddy. I'm not doin it. I'm not. I'm not doin it Mama.

I don't want to be anybody's wife. I don't want a husband. I'm not doin it Mama.

I am not tellin this baby's daddy.

He has big plans on what he's gonna do with his life, and I can tell you raisin a baby here in these hills isn't one of em. Even if he wants to be a daddy I'm not leavin this place. I don't want to live anywhere but here.

I don't want to be a wife. I think this baby will have a good life here with you and me, and that's all that matters.

I hear ya. I know you think every man has a right to know he's a daddy. I'm sure you're right Mama. But I'm not doin it. I'm not. I'm not doin it Mama.

Well, I wanna keep workin at the store until this baby's born. Save some money and get things ready around here.

I don't want anyone comin in here tellin me they are the daddy and I gotta do what they say. I don't want anyone tellin me what to do because they are the man of the house. I'm not doin it Mama.

Please Mama.

You told me there wasn't anything in the world that would cause you to stop lovin me. I need you Mama.

Even if you think I'm doin the wrong thing, I need you to prop me up. You always say nothin is forever and we can always change our minds. So maybe I will change my mind, but right now, I'm not doin it.

No, you're wrong. I'm not doin this on my own.

I have you.

I have Billy Wade and Ash.

I have Granny Faye, Grandpap and Petey lookin out for me on the other side of things.

I have my home here. I get to walk in the woods every day. I get to feel the wind against my face and tip my eyes to the sun. The water in the creek sings to me Mama. It fills my soul so fulla joy I could just leap outta my skin. This is where I want my baby to grow up.

I want this baby to dance in the butterfly field and chew on fresh mint from the yard. I want this baby to learn how to chop wood and dig post holes. I want this baby to catch frogs and lightnin bugs. To sit on the porch in the rain with you. I want this baby to be able to read books by the big Oak. Pray in Pastor John's church. Pick blackberries. Pull a big, red mater off the vine and take a bite. Let the juice run right offa the chin. Count the swallas in the yard and hear the angels singin in the woods.

I want this baby to call these hills home.

Please Mama. I've been thinkin about this alot. Please.

I love you Mama. Please listen to me Mama.

Daddy's not welcome round this baby either. You have to promise me, he's not allowed to be a Grandpap to this baby. Please Mama. I need you now more than ever.

Mama. Mama.

Please. Please Mama.

Thank you Mama.

• *Wendy Jett*

Notebook

Would the horse choose to wear the saddle?

Honeycomb

wrong chromosome   creek foam   pine tree dome
still as stone   seeds sown   broken bone   highest
throne   windsong tone   satan's gnome   storms
blown   tossed and thrown   funeral home   eternal
tomb   up and grown   all alone   run and roam
weighty tome   quarrelsome   quarrelsome

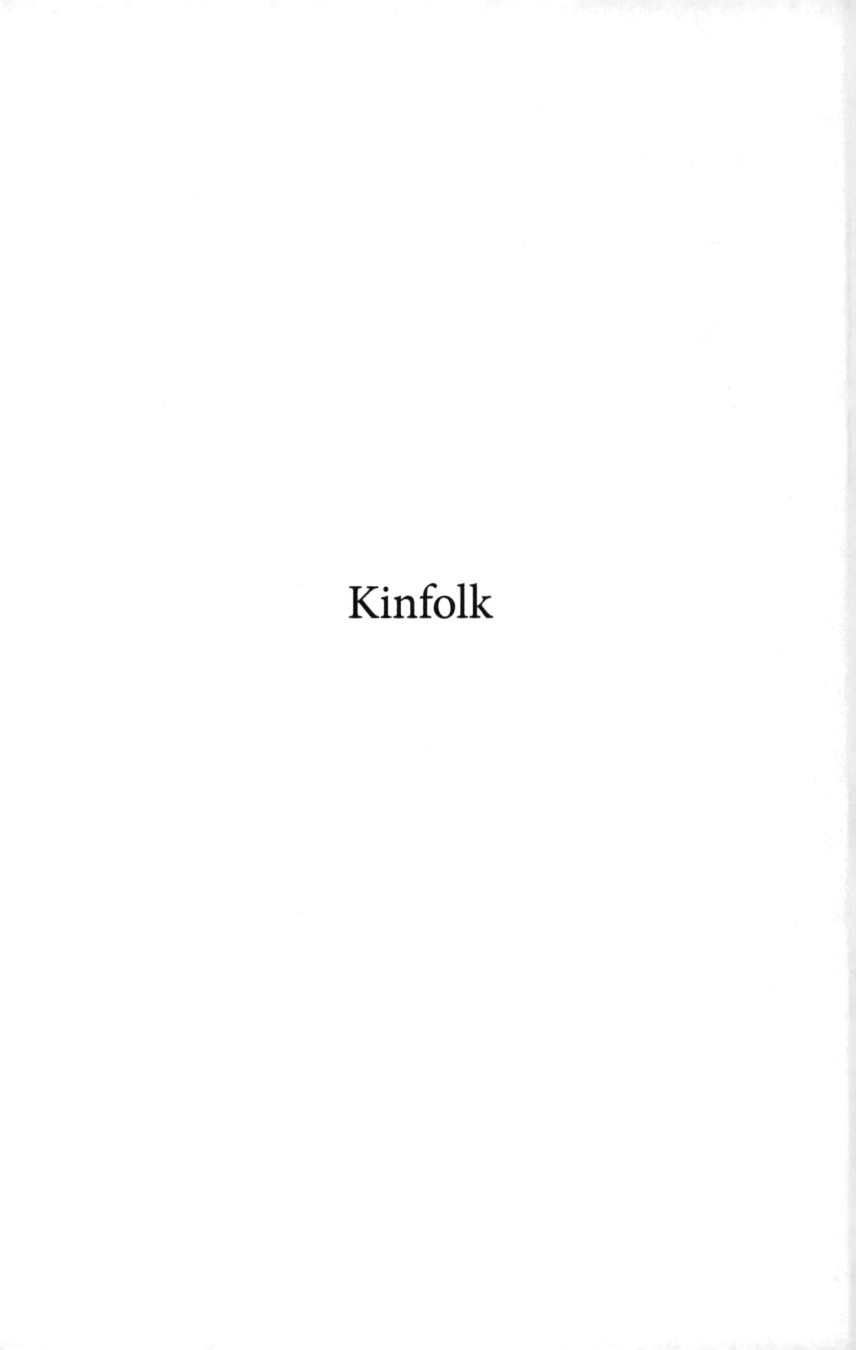

Kinfolk

BillyWade, Ash and Ms. Verna sure have been workin hard to keep Granny Faye's place lookin good. I don't think the barn's ever looked this clean. Grandpap would be happy about that. The front porch looks all fancy too with the table, chairs and flowerpots. I knock on the door, and Ash opens it with baby Trigg in her arms.

"C'mon in Girl, we been waitin for ya, haven't we Trigg?" Ash opens the door, and I can smell somethin cookin on the stove. Ms. Verna comes outta the kitchen with her apron on. "Well hey there Girl! Aren't you lookin good! I got me some beef stew on the stove, I hope you'll be stayin a bit and eat with us." Ms. Verna smiles and rubs her hands on her apron. "Here, I'll take that big boy for a bit, and you two can visit." Ash hands Trigg to Ms. Verna, and she goes back in the kitchen.

"Let's sit a spell. Hope you don't mind if I fold some of Trigg's clothes while we talk." Ash sits on the couch and pulls the laundry basket over to her feet. I tell her I'm happy to help too, so we start foldin little boy clothes.

"How you feelin bout bein a Mama? I know I was scared even though I was happy." Ash holds up a little pair of pajamas to me and smiles.

"Well to tell ya the truth, I'm not quite sure how I feel." I grab some baby socks and roll em into a ball. "I love babies and I love children, and I always thought I'd be a Mama some day, so I guess that's good. But I really wasn't thinkin it would be so soon. But I can tell you I really feel somethin like a miracle is happenin to my body. I can hardly believe I'm growin a human bein in my belly."

Ash laughs. "Ain't that the truth. Growin another whole person in your body is as strange as it is excitin." Ash starts foldin the tiniest pair of jeans I've ever seen. "Well, Girl I hope you know me and BillyWade are here to help ya. I know your Mama's there to help, but we are too. Ms. Verna too." Ash pats my hand. "BillyWade is always sayin you are his sister and the best friend he ever had. So don't you be worryin bout things. We will help you. I've always wanted a sister, so I figure me and you can help each other out."

I can feel my heart flippin around in my chest. "Oh Ash, thank you. I love you and BillyWade and baby Trigg too. I hope our babies can be life long friends." I give Ash's hands a squeeze. "And I sure hope I can borrow some of these baby clothes when it's time. They sure are cute."

The basket of laundry is folded, so Ash pushes it under the side table. About that time Ms. Verna comes outta the kitchen with Trigg. "I think this boy would like to take him a walk. Do you girls feel like takin him out a bit while I finish up my biscuits in the kitchen?"

Ash takes Trigg from Ms. Verna and turns to hand him off to me. "Here ya go Girl, you can practice wranglin a bull. See if you can get this jacket on him, and we'll take a quick walk."

Ash is right. Puttin Trigg in a jacket is like wranglin a bull or maybe even givin a cat a bath. But I got him in it. Ash pulls out a little baby stroller that looks like a motorcycle. Funniest thing I've ever seen! Ash rolls her eyes. "Ain't this funny?" She points to the stroller. "I think we really got it for BillyWade." We both laugh, and she gives the stroller a push out the front door. "Can ya help me lift him down the steps? He's gettin heavy." We pick up the stroller and walk down the three steps of Granny Faye's place. I know Granny's watchin. I can feel her lookin out the front winda.

Ash starts to push that little motorcycle down the front walk, then I hear her say, "C'mon Koga!" Sure enough Koga comes outta the tree and lands on the handle. "Let's take us a walk with our sister."

Life is good today. Yes, it is.

• *Wendy Jett*

Notebook

Some families are born by blood
Others by strangers bonded in love

Notebook

Asher BillyWade Creek
~~Daddy~~ Daisy   Expecting
Faye Grandpap Huckleberry
Innocence Jack Kinfolk
Love   Mama Nightfall
Oak   Petey   Quilt
Rocks Sunflower Trigg
Unfortunate Verna Woods
X that hole in my soul
Yesterday   Zilch

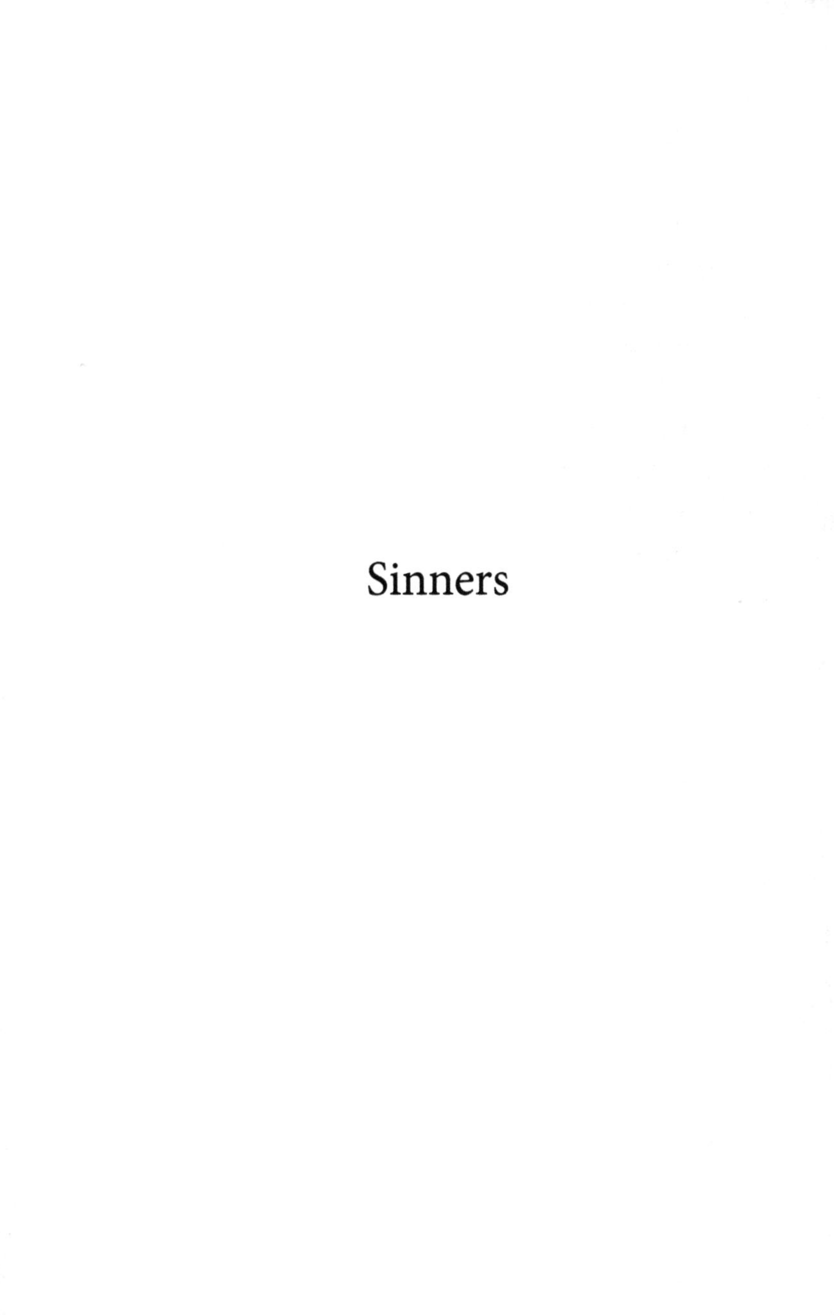

Sinners

I told Mama I didn't want to sit up front, but she won't have it any other way. She says God's word is stronger up front. I told her I can hear Pastor John just fine from the back. But here we sit. Front row.

I can feel every pair of eyes starin at the back of my head. I can hear all the judgements bein passed inside their hearts. It doesn't matter that Pastor is preachin from Matthew. "Do not judge, or you too will be judged." People always seem to think it's not about them. Mama says all the ones that need to listen and take it in the most seem to become deaf in church. She says the best thing we can do is listen to Pastor and not worry about others. Sometimes it's not that easy.

The sweat is rollin down the middle of my swollen chest onto my belly. It doesn't matter that it's not that hot outside. I'm glad the service is over. I tell Mama I'm goin on to the car, and she can stand in line to talk to Pastor. She always has to thank him for the sermon and bless him before she can go home.

Walkin down the four steps sure is alot easier than gettin up them, I'll say that. There's a group of ladies standin at the bottom. As I walk by I hear Pearly Coomer say, "It sure is a shame that baby ain't gonna have a daddy, and its mama is two shy of a dozen." I can feel myself start burnin down inside my bones. Then I hear Granny Faye's voice in my head say, "Pay them no mind. Just keep on walkin Girl." So I do. I stick my big ol belly out a bit more, pat it and walk on by.

Seems like I don't get ten steps away when I hear my Mama say, "Pearly Coomer, who do you think you are? Didn't you hear one word Pastor John said all mornin?" There's Mama toe to toe with Pearly. Course Pearly's two best friends are standin on each side of her starin at Mama like cats on a mouse.

"I didn't say nuthin that ain't true," Pearly snaps, then wipes the corner of her lipstick with her little finger. "That poor baby ain't got no chance of growin up good."

Mama doesn't even raise her voice but that look she carries in her eyes sure does change. "Now Pearly Coomer, you know my Girl is one of the most honest, carin, God lovin people in this county. This baby is a blessin to all us. I think you should spend some time lookin at your own child fore you throw them words at mine. Charlie's been nothin but a mean, name callin, rock throwin, lyin boy his whole life, but that don't surprise me none, you bein his Mama and all."

I grab Mama by the arm just in time. Pearly tosses a spit ball at Mama right outta that lipsticked mouth of hers. Pastor John comes skippin down the steps and jumps right into Pearly and her friends. Me and Mama laugh all the way to the car.

Course we get to the car and it has a flat tire. Mama says it's God's way of sayin he's not happy with her. I know we don't have a spare. It was flat, so I left it with Billy Wade to patch up. About that time, Daddy pulls his truck up right behind the car. "You girls need sum help?" He sticks his head outta the winda and gives Mama a wink. "I can take y'all home if you ain't got a spare."

"I'm not ridin with him. I'll walk home if I have to." I talk as clear as I can.

Mama says, "You can't be walkin home Girl. We can ride with your Daddy."

The Lord must be lookin out for me because Jack Perry pulls up right behind Daddy. "Good mornin ladies. Can I help ya out?" Jack smiles and opens his truck door. Daddy is not happy about it.

"I can take these girls home," Daddy talks a little louder than he needs to. "We're family. They're goin with me."

"I told you, I'm not ridin with you, and Mama's not ridin with you either." I try to talk louder than Daddy and make sure I look him right in the eyes.

Mama whispers to me. "I'll go with Daddy Girl. Sumtimes it's easier to just go along fore things get outta hand." Then Mama turns to Daddy and says, "Well Girl why don't you ride home with Jack, and I'll ride with your Daddy. That way everybody is happy, and me and your Daddy can talk about this new grandbaby comin."

I whisper to Mama, "I don't want him anywhere around this baby. You hear me."

"Sounds good to me!" Daddy smiles and leans over to open the door for Mama. "Climb in woman. We got some talkin to do."

Mama gives me a nod and says, "I'll be just fine Girl. See you at home." She shuts the door, and Daddy lets the truck start to roll.

"You take her right home now, you hear me?" I yell at Daddy as he pulls away.

Jack opens the truck door for me and helps me climb in. "Thanks Jack. We gotta get home quick. I don't trust my Daddy any farther than I can run these days."

Jack laughs and starts the engine. "Don't you worry, Girl. I'll take care of ya. I'll get you home to your Mama and that Possum of yours quick enough."

Woman

She smells like earth.
Rich, dense with life.

Yet sadness has burrowed
into her bones. Fingers wilted
flowers. Ears twisted hollow tree
trunks. Rivers pour from her mouth.
Flowing swirling rolling across the
swollen hill of her belly. There in
the corner of her eye. A broken
branch of hope floats
down her cheek.

She smells like earth.
Rich, dense with life.

Preach

brothers and sisters i say unto you judge not or you too shall be judged judge not or you too shall be judged for in the same way you judge others you will be judged almighty god tells you do not condemn the speck of sawdust in your neighbors eye but then pay no attention to the full plank in your own eye yes the full plank in your own eye brothers i say judge not those who talk bad about you when your own mouth speaks words of condemnation sisters i say sisters do not judge those that give in to earthly temptations when your own heart whispers desire for forbidden fruit do not pass these judgements upon your brothers your sisters your neighbors your kin instead reach your hand yes reach your hand to those who struggle open your heart the heart your lord gave you open it to those that need help to those that walk this path with us do not judge or you too you too shall be judged my brothers my sisters shall be judged yes judgment day is comin i say unto you judgement day is a comin

Water

Well, Possum, I'm sure this is the only time a whale has been in this county. Yep, I'm sure this creek has never seen a whale before. I'm hot, I gotta put my feet in the water. Sure feels good. Cold, soft mud squishin up in my toes. I'd say I am about as big as a whale these days. Yes, Ma'am. This baby needs to get here before my belly just splits wide open.

Looky there Possum. A monarch butterfly! What a beauty she is. Wings so big I do believe she'd give you a ride if you asked her nicely. I'm gonna sit myself down here on this table rock. Get me some sun. There's nothin like the sun and creek to fill your spirit.

What are we gonna name this baby, Possum? What do you think? Boy or girl? Doesn't really matter to me. I'm gonna love this baby just because it's mine. I know you're gonna love it too, aren't ya? You know you're so ugly you're cute. Yes you are.

I sat on this same rock with Petey a few times. Mama didn't really like him comin to this part of the creek. Water gets a bit deep. She was always scared of one of us drownin since her Grandpap drown in the river. One time we sat on this rock and watched a mama coon and her babies climb a tree. Looked like they were havin fun gettin in some good trouble.

My back is hurtin a bit today. Baby must be layin on my bones or somethin. What do you hear girl? It's ok, there's nothin around here that's gonna hurt us.

"Well, if it ain't a bathin beauty and her possum." Jack Perry steps over the rottin tree stump. "You girls enjoyin a day off today I guess."

"Hey there Jack. We thought we'd take a little dip and get some sun before this baby comes. My back's been hurtin today, so I thought I'd sit a spell first. What are you doin down here?" I cup my hands and grab some water. Toss it on the back of my neck.

"I'm just gettin me a few good, big, flat rocks. Makin me a path all the way from the yard to the creek, seein I'm at the creek most days. Thought I'd make it easier to get up and down. Got my pull wagon over there fulla rocks. Just need a couple more." Jack bends over and scoops Possum up. "You're sure an ugly little thing ain't you?" Jack gives Possum a kiss right on the top of her head.

I toss another scoop of water on the back of my neck. "Shoulda brought me some water to drink. It's hotter than I thought. I'm not feelin too good Jack. I best be headin back home."

"I got some water in the wagon. Stay right there I'll get ya some." Jack puts Possum in my lap and heads to the wagon. About that time a big old bullfrog jumps right on top of the rock. Possum jumps off my lap at the frog. The frog hops right back in the water, and Possum jumps in after it.

"Possum! Get back up here! What are you doin!" I roll to one side on my knees and pull Possum back up on the rock. Jack comes runnin through the brush.

"Well, I can't leave you two for a minute without you findin trouble. Everythin ok?" Jack has the thermos of water in his hand.

I tuck one foot under my belly and push myself up off my knees so I can stand. "Whew, that's harder than it used ta be! I'll take that drink, thanks Jack." I reach out for the thermos, but before I can grab it, a rush of water splashes down on the rock from right between my legs. "Oh Lord Jack. I think this baby's comin. We best get back home."

"Let's get you in the wagon! I can pull you up the hill! Let's go! Let's go!" Jack starts actin like he's been stung by a hornet. Jumpin all around.

"I can walk Jack. It's ok, it doesn't happen that fast. Let's walk up the hill to your place then you can take me and Possum to Doc Andrews. C'mon Possum, let's get movin." I can feel a lump in my throat, and my legs are shakin, but I do my best to give Jack a smile.

Mermaid

i swim
      my mother's
            ocean
      ears awash
in the rhythm
  of her heart
maternal blood
      streams past
          generous bountiful
      submerged within
i navigate
  her canal
        flutter
            bob
        kick
emerge with the
  mouth of a fish
        open wide in terror
    gulping
   for that first
        breath

• *Wendy Jett*

Redemption

i
  did not know that when

      i
        birthed my child

            i
              would also be   reborn

Homecomin

"Ruby Faye is a perfect name for her." Billy Wade turns down the radio. "I never seen a newborn with so much curly hair and red to beat. I'd say Ruby fits her just fine."

I think Billy Wade's right. Ruby Faye is the perfect name for her. There's nothin prettier than a ruby out in the sun, and there's nothin stronger than my Granny Faye. I'd say Ruby and Faye make a recipe for a good life.

"I sure appreciate you takin me and Ruby home from the hospital Billy Wade. Mama's still workin on gettin Ruby's space together." I tuck Ruby's blanket up round her toes. She keeps kickin her feet out.

"Ain't no problem at all, Girl. Ash took Trigg and my Mama over to pick up sum books at the library. That takes em bout all day. Cause you know you bout hafta pull my Mama outta there with a tractor." Billy Wade smiles and winks at me. Billy Wade is a good man.

The truck bounces up over the edge between Highway 25 and home. Life sure has changed these past few months, but I guess life is always changin if you think about it. Mama says the only thing you can really count on in life is that it will change. She says the best thing you can do to be happy in life is just to decide you're gonna be happy. Waitin on things to get set straight will just keep you waitin forever. Just decide to be happy where you are with what you have, and you will be happy. I'm happy right now.

"I hafta tell you, Miss Ruby Faye is gonna be a force round these parts! Ain't ya girl?" BillyWade laughs and rubs Ruby's hand. "That mark of birth right there proves it! She's special. Ain't no hidin that!" I'd say BillyWade's right. Any baby born with a mark of birth is special. But a dragonfly mark of birth. That's an angel's kiss. Ruby's dragonfly sits on the back of her left hand, just past her wrist bone. I'd say Petey had somethin to do with that. She is special.

BillyWade slows down so we can pull up the drive. "Hey, ain't that your daddy's truck?" BillyWade points out the winda. There sits Daddy's truck pulled up by the front steps. Possum is on the front porch barkin and runnin back and forth across the front of the house.

BillyWade stops the truck. I can hear Mama yellin. I can hear Daddy yellin. Possum is barkin. BillyWade says, "Sumthins wrong!" He pushes open the truck door, and then

a single gunshot.

The entire world goes silent.

Completely   silent.

BillyWade seems to be lifted out of the truck in slow motion. I watch the dirt puff up under his boot. It floats in the air like a lost balloon. Driftin up and away. Then it disappears. He steps toward the porch. Stops. Turns to me, his mouth moves. Open, close, open, close, open, close. He is a mockingbird with no voice .

I smell a hint of honeysuckle in my nose. I take a deep breath. Hold it tight in my lungs. The sun is warm on my face. I can feel the space between my toes.

All I can do is stare at the lone blue dragonfly on the windshield. Light streaks through its wings. They look like four stained glass windas. It tilts its head to one side as if to say, "I see you Girl."

Then I hear myself singin.

Dragonfly, dragonfly, Angels sing
Angels a sittin on a dragonfly wing

Dragonfly, dragonfly, Angels sing
Angels a sittin on a dragonfly wing

Dragonfly

Dragonfly

Angels

Sing

Death

did not knock

it simply
slithered
under the door

disguised as a
warm summer breeze

• *Wendy Jett*

Sacrament

life burns tenDer flesh

cAlloused trembling hands craDle salt jar
one pinch between finger anD thumb
press deeplY into smoldering tissue

yesterday's pain screams in silence

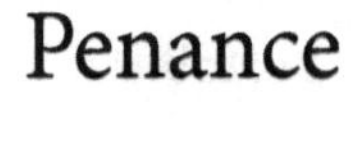

Penance

Mama shot him. Once. That's all it took. Not sure if he is in heaven or hell. I think maybe he is just walkin somewhere in between with that millstone wrapped around his neck for all the bad things he did. Mama's all tore up about it. She will never get over it. She's good at forgivin others, but she's never gonna forgive herself.

Doc Andrews said her broken ribs and nose will heal. He said that God works in mysterious ways and that this was one of them. Mama's cancer is back. Doc said that we probably wouldn't have known it was back until it was too late if it weren't for the fact that Mama got beat and had to be looked over. Sounds like Doc Andrews is tryin to make a skunk a cat, but it doesn't matter. All that matters is Mama healin. Inside and out.

Mama says her cancer came back the minute she pulled that trigger. Says it's her penance for shootin Daddy. I think Mama's wrong. God doesn't work that way. He's not gonna make Mama suffer just for her protectin herself. God doesn't make people sick. He doesn't want anyone to suffer. I think it hurts his heart to watch his people suffer. Sickness and sufferin are just part of what we have to deal with in this human body we got. But we also get to feel the sun on our face, and smell fresh bread bakin and hold our babies in our arms. I'd say it's all a blessin if you look at it that way. Like Mama says, you just gotta decide to be happy where you are with what you have.

I feel a bit guilty sayin that Daddy bein off this earth has made me feel lighter. But it has. I can take some deep breaths for the first time in a long while. I don't hafta worry anymore about Daddy beatin on Mama or him gettin to me or him throwin Ruby against the wall like he did Petey. I don't hafta worry about his truck bein in the drive or round the corner from the store or pullin up to the church. I don't have to worry any more about him standin out there in the middle of night by the big Oak, talkin to all his boy babies. I don't even hafta think about my Daddy if I don't want to.

I know someday Ruby Faye's gonna ask about her Grandpap. Not sure what I'm gonna say about him. I have time to figure that out I guess. Time to pray for God's guidance. I know Mama will tell me that I need to forgive Daddy for all the bad things he did in his life. I don't know that I will ever be able to do that. I just don't know.

Right now, I need to spend my time carin for Mama and Ruby. I know that we're gonna be ok. We've been through many a storm before. This one isn't any different. The darker the storm, the brighter the rainbow, and I see the clouds partin right now. It's gonna be ok Mama. It's all gonna be ok.

• *Wendy Jett*

Ghost

muted weeping from deep
in the wood | soft muffled
whimpers | cross gurgling
creek | past whispering cattail |
narrow stark path of dirt |
follow stifled cries | weeds |
vines | dull wails | rocks | roots |

there

sprawled atop rotted
poplar stump | one
Mourning Dove feather
sobs |

Unholy

Earthworms
from bloody apples
weave
threads of justice.

Birthdays

One

Mama yells through the front screen door. "Girl, Jack, c'mon out here on the porch! I got somethin to show ya!"

Mama's sittin in the rocker with Ruby Faye on her lap. Possum's stretched out in the sun on the porch step. It's a perfect day for a birthday party. Jack opens the screen and holds it for me as I wipe my hands on my apron. Pink icing stuck to my nails.

"Listen here! Listen here!" Ruby is facin Mama so Mama gives her a big old grin. Ruby Faye laughs. Curls bouncin. "Who do you love Ruby Faye? Who do you love? Tell your Granny. C'mon now." Ruby Faye just smiles. "C'mon now, Ruby. Tell your Granny. Who do you love? Can you say Granny? Who do you love? Say Granny."

Ruby opens her mouth wide as a bass and says, "NeeNee". Mama lifts her up in the air. "That's my girl! Did you hear that? Her first word is Granny! Yes, it is!"

Jack gives me a wink. "Yes, ma'am. It sure was Granny!"

Two

I tip my head back and whisper through the screen on the front winda. "Mama, you have to take a peek at this. Looky out here."

"Girl can't it wait? I'm bout done mendin these pants."

"No, it can't wait. Don't make any noise, but come look out the screen door."

Mama gets up and tiptoes to the screen. "Well, I'll be. I never seen nuthin like that before." Mama smiles. "She sure is a special one, ain't she?"

There sits Ruby Faye on the top step of the porch. Possum sittin next to her on one side and a big, fat, black crow sittin on the other side. They are all just lookin out over the yard as she shares her piece of birthday cake with em.

Mama says, "Looks like our Ruby got herself a crow for her birthday."

Three

BillyWade is chasin Trigg and Ruby Faye cross the yard. Possum is bringin up the caboose, yelpin like a chicken.

"C'mon BillyWade, the cake is ready! C'mon Trigg! C'mon Ruby Faye, you gotta blow out your candles!" Mama yells from the porch and claps her hands. BillyWade picks up Trigg under one arm and Ruby Faye under the other.

"I got me two big sacks of rotten taters! Where you want em Girl? Should I toss em in the sinkhole?" BillyWade laughs and spins in a circle.

Ash steps out on the porch and puts her arm around my shoulder. "Well, looks like we got us three children playin in the yard, don't it?" She laughs, and BillyWade runs up the steps with Possum on his heels.

BillyWade yells, "Let's get us some cake fore Jack eats it all!"

I'd say today is a happy day. It sure is.

Four

Mama and Ruby have been sittin on the porch all mornin. Rain rumblin and pourin off the roof. Ruby has a new birthday drawin notebook and crayons. Mama's been putin down some embroidery on pillacases she made. Flowers with ladybugs and dragonflies. Sure is pretty. Mama's been hummin a bit off and on. Hymns mostly. To be honest, I didn't know I could be this happy. My life is as full as the rain barrel today.

Jack says, "We best set the table. BillyWade, Ash and Trigg'll be here soon. I can't wait to meet baby Knox. I bet he looks just like BillyWade."

I give Jack a wink and say, "let's hope he has some of his mama in there too."

Five

Ruby Faye's been carryin a frog round the house all day. She named him Hopper. Even made a little song about him for Mama. Been singin it at the top of her lungs all day long. "Hopper the frog. He's a little toad. Hopper the frog. Found em on the road. Hopper the frog. He can jump so high. Hopper the frog. He can even fly. Fly away frog. Fly away. Fly away frog. Fly away."

Mama says, "C'mon over here to NeeNee Ruby Faye. Let me see that frog. I do believe he has wings." Ruby skips over to Mama and sits next to her on the porch step. "You are so smart to sing that little song. You are old beyond your years Ruby. Well, he sure does have some of them little wing buds growin up under his arms. I think we got us a special frog here." Ruby Faye tips her head back, "I knew it NeeNee! I knew it! He can fly! He's special!"

Mama says, "Yes he is Ruby Faye. He is special. Just like you and your Mama. You are both special girls to me. Yes, you are." Mama gives Ruby a big squeeze, then gives me one of them looks she carries in her eyes. The kind that talks without sayin anything.

"Mama, are you ok? Mama, what's wrong?" I sit down next to her and Ruby.

"Mama. Mama. What's wrong?"

Departed

there came a day
i did not wake
for i was busy
loving
those i had
spent years
grieving

• *Wendy Jett*

Graveyard

i will not etch
your name cross
limestone slab

for it has already
taken root within
my heart

Mama

Dear Mama,

I can't believe it's been a whole year since you left us. My heart's not healed yet. Not sure it will ever heal. I really thought that cancer was gone for good. It's been hard without you Mama. I want to turn around and ask you about how to be a good Mama to Ruby, but you're not there. I hope you hear me talking to you in my prayers. I hope you are watching over us.

I'm sure everyone was so happy to see you at the gates of heaven. I pray you are spending some time with Granny and Grandpap and that you're getting to hug on Petey and your other boy babies. You waited a long time to be a Mama to them.

You are the strongest woman I've ever known Mama. Your soul must have been so full of holes with losing both your parents and your boy babies. But you still kept on taking care of Ruby Faye and me. Kept on loving us hard everyday. Strong and righteous, yes you are.

Our little Miss Ruby Faye is doing pretty good. She started back at school a couple months ago. Possum sits on the porch all day waiting for her to come home, and that crow of hers just sits in the school yard like Koga did for Ash. Ruby talks to you every night when we say her prayers. I hope you can hear her Mama. She sure does miss you.

She is a mover that one is. She still loves the creek and climbing trees. She found a box turtle the other day. Named him Lightnin. You'd be happy to know Ruby and Trigg are still peas in a pod. He really watches over her. She's a bit wilder than him, so I'm glad he reels her in at times. I think they will be lifelong friends.

Jack Perry and BillyWade put a new roof on the house. They're going to put one on Granny Faye's house too. They are both good men, Mama. They've been good to Ruby Faye and me. I know we are lucky to have them in our lives.

I've been thinking about going back to school to finish up my teaching degree like you wanted me to, but to tell you the truth Mama, I love my life like it is. I love these glorious hills, the sound of the creek jumping across the rock, the smell of the leaves tossed in the wind. The only thing I don't like is that you are not here, and I know that feeling won't ever go away. I keep hoping I will see you out at the big Oak one night. You and Granny Faye. I'll keep looking for you Mama.

Oh, how I miss you Mama. I feel like I'm always gonna have a piece of me missing. Always. Thank you for being such a good Mama to me and a wonderful NeeNee to Ruby Faye.

I'm gonna fold this letter up and burn it in the fireplace like Ash told me to do. She said it's sure to get to you in heaven that way. I am praying she is right.

• *Wendy Jett*

I love you now and forever Mama.

Your Girl,
Rose Ellen

Acknowledgments

First and foremost, thank you Katerina Stoykova for believing that GIRL's story deserved to be heard. Your support has enriched my life in so many ways.

A special thanks to Kathleen Gregg, Marcia Thornton Jones, Sylvia Ahrens, Missy Brownson Ross and Mike Wilson for taking time to read Girl's stories and write an endorsement. I respect and value each of you so very much.

… and finally, a huge thank you to ALL who have supported GIRL's story. I love hearing your input after you read her words! Your kindness has been overwhelming.

The roots of love run deep, yes they do.

About the Author

Wendy Jett is a longtime fitness instructor, decoupage nerd, improv junkie and loves to write. She is a born and raised Kentucky girl who now calls Lexington home. Mom to two humans, Kayla and Stevie, and one canine, Lola Jolene, she does the best she can every day. Some days she does better than others. Rumor has it that she can be bribed with peanut M&M's. You can reach her at wendyjett@rocketmail.com

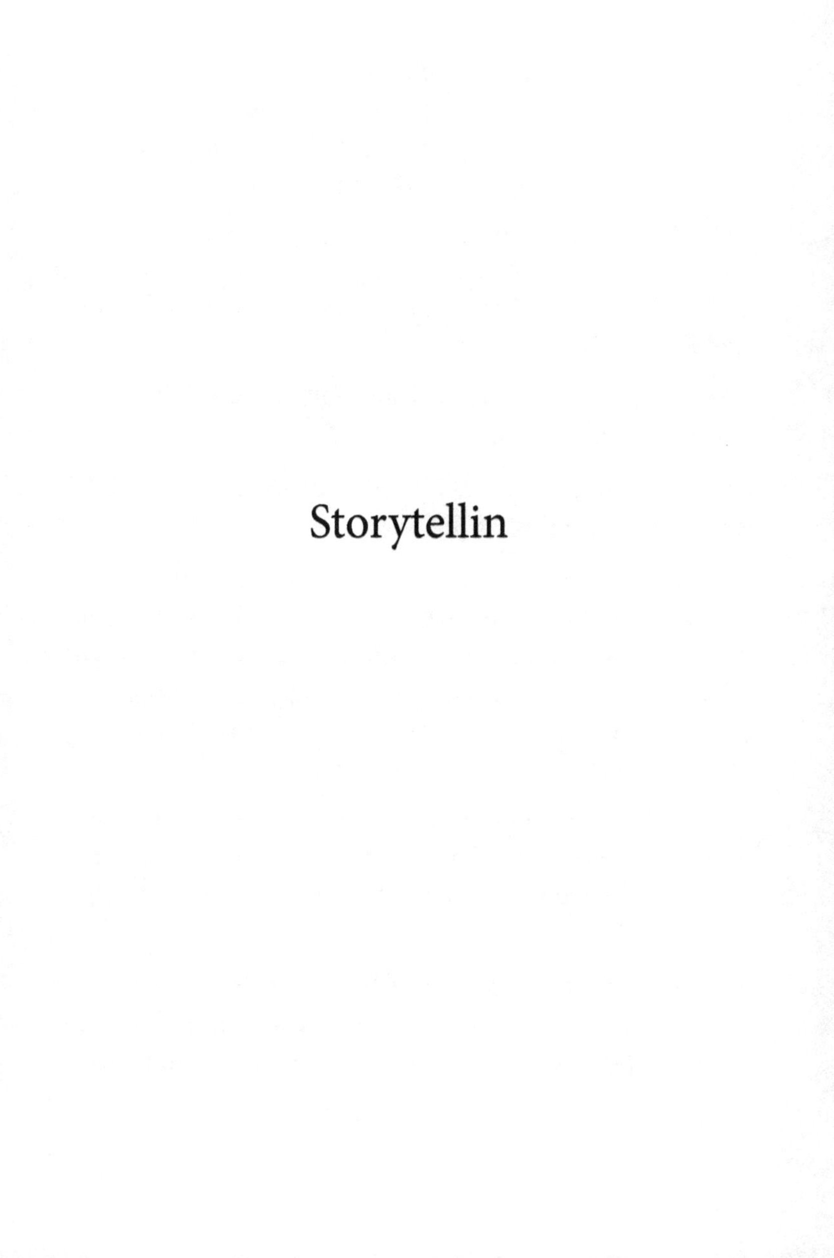

Storytellin

"Please Mama. Please. Tell me the story bout when you was born. Tell me bout NeeNee and Granny Faye. Please." Ruby Faye snuggles in a little closer on the couch and lays her legs right cross the top of mine.

"Oh, Ruby Faye, you heard that story many a time. You don't wanna hear that old thing again do you?" I push her red curls out of her eyes. Those green emeralds look right up at me.

"Yes Mama! Yes! Please!" Ruby pulls Possum onto the couch and into her lap.

"Ok, one more time.… I'll tell you the story of when I was born into this world.

The only time an elephant was in this county was the year I was born. Well, that's what NeeNee said. She said she was big as an elephant when she was carryin me. Ankles all swole up, face fat as a well-fed hog. Biggest pregnant woman this side of the Mississippi. Granny Faye called her "Big Mama" til the day I was born.

I came burstin outta her body, screamin like a skinned rabbit. NeeNee said that was the best day of her life. All she ever wanted was a baby girl. She got what she wanted. Me.

Course my Daddy wanted a boy. Somebody to shoot with. Somebody to help work on the truck. Somebody to set fence posts. I told my Daddy hundreds of time, I can shoot. I can work on the truck. I can dig post holes. My Daddy just said, "Git Girl. Go find your Mama."

www.ingramcontent.com/pod-product-compliance
Lightning Source LLC
Chambersburg PA
CBHW031413310726
48971CB00003B/851